Accepted

PRAISE FOR *STORYSHARES*

"One of the brightest innovators and game-changers in the education industry."
– Forbes

"Your success in applying research-validated practices to promote literacy serves as a valuable model for other organizations seeking to create evidence-based literacy programs."

- Library of Congress

"We need powerful social and educational innovation, and Storyshares is breaking new ground. The organization addresses critical problems facing our students and teachers. I am excited about the strategies it brings to the collective work of making sure every student has an equal chance in life."
– Teach For America

"Around the world, this is one of the up-and-coming trailblazers changing the landscape of literacy and education."
- International Literacy Association

"It's the perfect idea. There's really nothing like this. I mean wow, this will be a wonderful experience for young people."   - Andrea Davis Pinkney, Executive Director, Scholastic

"Reading for meaning opens opportunities for a lifetime of learning. Providing emerging readers with engaging texts that are designed to offer both challenges and support for each individual will improve their lives for years to come. Storyshares is a wonderful start."
- David Rose, Co-founder of CAST & UDL

Accepted

John Smistad

STORYSHARES

Story Share, Inc.
New York. Boston. Philadelphia

Storyshares
Story Share, Inc.
24 N. Bryn Mawr Avenue #340
Bryn Mawr, PA 19010-3304
www.storyshares.org

Inspiring reading with a new kind of book.

Interest Level: High School
Grade Level Equivalent: 3.4

9781642615425

Book design by Storyshares

Printed in the United States of America

Storyshares Presents

1

"So, you up for it, big guy?" the leader asks me.

"Yeah. I'm up for it. Hell *yeah* I'm up for it, man!" I say.

I'm trying for forceful. Instead, my delivery is forced.

These are "The Chosen Ones." "The Ruling Class." To be one of them, a guy like me would give up a kidney.

It turns out that's not the asking price.

I'm a "Blender." It's my high school's label for people who fade into the background. People who barely register in the teenage kingdom.

People who are pointless.

But after years of being ignored, that's all about to change.

"Awesome. We'll see you Saturday night. Ten o'clock. Beacon Point Park. Make-Out Grove," the leader says. He's also the handsome soccer team captain.

He steps toward me. He leans in close enough for me to smell the brandy on his breath.

He adds, "And you better not keep us waiting. Got that, stud?"

"Yeah. I got it," I say.

Looking down, I stare at the gap between the hem of his khaki pants and his brown leather shoes. He isn't wearing socks. That's how you roll when you're one of the Chosen Ones.

Done deal.

2

I first met Darlene last fall in my Earth Sciences class. She's quiet. She keeps to herself. Just like me. And she's super smart. Unlike me.

We sat next to each other. We teamed up for our midterm project, "What's So Hard About Rocks?" We got along great. Our project earned an A-.

Last week, I asked Darlene if she might want to go downtown with me. I was going to listen to a speech by a conservative politician.

Darlene said that she tended to "lean left," but she thought it would be an interesting experience. I took this to mean that she might at least tolerate me.

I didn't know that we had been overheard talking. Later that day, I was offered the proposal.

So, I pick Darlene up at her house.

She introduces me to her parents. They're nice people. Quiet. Bookish. The apple definitely didn't fall far from the trees.

As we pull out of her driveway, I steal a look at Darlene. Her short, brown hair is pulled back in a ponytail with a tie-dyed scrunchie. She's wearing her usual horn-rimmed glasses. I always imagine that she's even prettier without them.

We don't say much on the drive to the Civic Arena. "I can't stand that teacher." "I love this song." "Cold outside, huh?" Simple, first-date stuff.

Darlene has no idea what's to come.

The speech is actually pretty cool. The politician is definitely preaching to the choir. Still, there's something inspiring about the whole thing. Darlene agrees, though not strongly.

My excuse for going off-route on the way back to Darlene's house is lame.

"We'll get a way better view of the sky and all those stars," I say. "And it's only about an extra ten minutes."

Beacon Point Park is a mile ahead.

My palms are gushing with sweat. Butterflies dive-bomb my stomach. I can't swallow. Talking is impossible.

Half a mile to go.

My eyes dart toward Darlene. She looks so… happy.

My mind is on autopilot. Time stops. Everything's gone silent.

A gentle voice pierces the stillness.

"I had a good time tonight," Darlene says.

I choke on my answer. "So did I."

Accepted

3

They are waiting.

They're hiding behind bushes and trees. Wearing Halloween masks. Made bolder by cases of imported beer.

They've got all the latest devices to record high-res pictures and videos. They're waiting to blast social media with images that will change two lives forever.

The park entrance is on the right.

I'm shaking my head. Darlene must be wondering why.

I keep on driving.

I point at the windshield toward a flash in the darkness. "Check it out," I say. "Shooting stars."

Darlene takes off her glasses, pushing them on top of her head. She looks through the window.

"Oh, wow. Cool," she says. She smiles. "You're right. These stars are amazing. Thanks so much for taking the 'long way' home."

Tonight was about a bargain. To be accepted.

Done deal.

About The Author

John Smistad is a contributing author to the Storyshares library.

About The Publisher

Story Shares is a nonprofit focused on supporting the millions of teens and adults who struggle with reading by creating a new shelf in the library specifically for them. The ever-growing collection features content that is compelling and culturally relevant for teens and adults, yet still readable at a range of lower reading levels.

Story Shares generates content by engaging deeply with writers, bringing together a community to create this new kind of book. With more intriguing and approachable stories to choose from, the teens and adults who have fallen behind are improving their skills and beginning to discover the joy of reading. For more information, visit storyshares.org.

Easy to Read. Hard to Put Down.

Accepted

www.ingramcontent.com/pod-product-compliance
Lightning Source LLC
Chambersburg PA
CBHW071232170626
46809CB00005BA/2044